D1511562

Downward Mule

Tree

Crow

Cat

Cow

Donkey

Handstand

Criss-Cross Applesauce

Sheep

To believers little and big. Namaste Chase, Brady, Jack and mom, my bona fide Lila.

~ J.H.

For Yasmin and Luke, my inspirations. Love you both.

~ S.P.

DOWNWARD MULE

WRITTEN BY
JENNA HAMMOND

ILLUSTRATED BY
STEVE PAGE

MacLaren-Cochrane Publishing

Hi. I'm Sam.

My mom is a horse. My dad is a donkey.
That makes me a mule.

I live in a barnyard. But I'm different from the farm animals.
I'm not speedy like Mom.
I move slower than a mower.

I'm not sturdy like Dad.
I hobble with a wobble.

I can't lay eggs like the hens. Or give milk like
the cows. I don't leap like the goats. Or share
fleece like the sheep.

On the one hoof, others tease me.
"Sam is slow."
"Shaky."
"Stubborn."
"Shy."

On the other hoof, they don't *really* know me.
I'm a secret yogi.

Just ask the farmer's daughter.
When the sun rises,
I yawn and stretch.
Lila rolls out her mat.

"Hello day," we say.
Then we breathe. Deep in. Deep out.
"Om!"

Our first pose is DOWNWARD MULE.

We both stand tall. TREE POSE.
It helps to stare at a tree for balance.

We flow to CROW. It gives me confidence.

Rooster wakes on cue. "Cock-a-doodle-doo!"
Of course, he can't see Lila and me.
We practice behind the barn.

We creep into CAT. "Meow."

Then COW. "Moo."

We whisper, "Namaste" and bow.

Big kick back. DONKEY POSE. "Hee-haw."

I finish in hoofstand. Lila tries HANDSTAND.

"Sam, you're a yoga superstar! Don't be stubborn. Show off who you are."

Lila asks every day. Always I neigh and bray,
"No way."
"Nope."
"No can do."
"You're nuts."
I don't have the guts to show my stuff.

Sometimes I practice alone in the shadows.
Then I'm hidden from everyone, even Lila.
Sun up. Sun salutations. Sundown.

"Oh my, did the cows just mosey by?"
Lila glares, "Who cares?"

Me.

"Why are you sitting funny?" Brown Cow moos.
"Sam, you're a silly mule."

The cows are unhappy.
The heat spoils their milk.

It makes the sheep too tired to give fleece.

The goats feel weak in the knees.

The hens can't lay an egg. *Clonk.*

What's a mule to do?

"Help the animals with yoga," Lila pleas.
"If not for them, do it for me.
There's nothing to bring to the farmer's market.
The barnyard is bare."

"OK," I bray. "Who's first?"
"The sheep," Lila points.
"The others will follow the flock."

I inch close. "SHEEP POSE."
One, two, three... Counting sheep, I see they copy me.
"Baa-ahh," we breathe.

WARRIOR ONE is a breeze.

For WARRIOR TWO and THREE
the goats stand by.
They need to modify.

"Try GOAT POSE.
Only don't lock horns with your neighbor."

"Neat," Billy Goat bleats. "I feel stronger."
His grin makes me hold it longer.

Mom and Dad circle around.

"Ready? Keep steady." HORSE.

Mom neighs, "Well done, Sam.

Great stretch for my galloping gams."

Dad adds, "And my hams."

The chicks cluck, "Can we try our luck?"
DUCK. Waddle, waddle.
"Quack!"
Squatting in the pose Mother Hen lays an egg.

The pigs shuffle in. "Can we begin?"
HAPPY BABY.
It's like wallowing in the mud.
Rooster puffs his chest.
"That all you got, Mule?"

What now? PLOW. "It's fine to wobble," I say.
"It's a yoga practice."

Rooster cock-a-doodles loud. I feel proud.

"Next it's DOWNWARD MULE."
I reach out and down. Then I look around.
Everyone is doing barnyard yoga.

Lila coos, "They want to be yogis too."
Be like me? For real?
My heart soars in WHEEL.

The mooing folk do COW.
Lila rushes down udder.
They fill more milk pails than she can count.

"Breathe in, breathe out," I shout! "RELAXATION now."
Everyone knows how. Lying down, we watch the clouds above.

Lila beams, "Now I've got a bounty for the market."
My new friends bow and say,

"Namaste."

Jenna Hammond ~ Author

For school visits and appearances see
jennahammondauthor.com

Jenna Hammond is a freelance writer and editor. Like Sam, she's also a closet yogi. Before parenthood, she led family yoga classes on weekends with a weekday desk job as editor-in-chief. Writing about a girl with special needs who walks because of yoga motivated Jenna's children's yoga certification. She holds a master's degree in journalism from New York University and a bachelor's degree in English with a minor in French from the University of Michigan. Find her on the beaches and ranches of Montauk, or the occasional barnyard on family travels.

Steve Page ~ Illustrator

stevepage.carbonmade.com

For as long as he can remember, Steve has had a pencil in his hand. With this love of drawing it was only natural that he would follow a career in the arts. After many successful years as a graphic designer, working for a variety of publishing companies, he decided to follow his heart and do what he loves most ~ create weird and wacky characters. When he is not drawing, which isn't very often, Steve likes to volunteer his time at his local primary school, where he encourages young minds to explore their creativity through drawing and painting. He's an animated movie fan and hopes that maybe one day one of his characters will play a leading role.

MacLaren-Cochrane Publishing

Downward Mule

© 2017 Text By Jenna Hammond

© 2017 Illustrations By Steve Page

MacLaren-Cochrane Publishing, PO BOX 6390, Folsom, CA 95763-6390

For orders visit:
www.maclaren-cochranepublishing.com
www.facebook.com/maclaren-cochranepublishing

Library of Congress Control Number: 2017901333

First Edition

ISBN:
HC: 978-1-365-44567-5
SC: 978-1-365-44564-4

Warrior 1

Warrior 2

Warrior 3

Goat

Horse Stance

Duck

Happy Baby

Plow

Wheel

Relaxation

Namaste

CPSIA information can be obtained at www.ICGtesting.com
Printed in the USA
BVIW12n1121080517
482493BV00015B/14